Gary Pau

World of Ac

Perfect Danger

MACMILLAN CHILDREN'S BOOKS

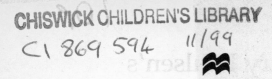

First published 1996 by Bantam Doubleday Dell, USA,
as *Project: A Perfect World*

First published in the UK 1999 by Macmillan Children's Books
a division of Macmillan Publishers Limited
25 Eccleston Place, London SW1W 9NF
Basingstoke and Oxford
www.macmillan.co.uk

Associated companies throughout the world

ISBN 0 330 37143 6

A CIP catalogue record for this book is available
from the British Library

Printed and bound in Great Britain by Mackays of Chatham plc, Kent

CHAPTER 1

"We're almost there, Jimbo." Jim Stanton's father grinned at him in the rearview mirror.

His mother turned sideways in the front seat of their old brown station wagon and gave her sandy-haired son an encouraging smile. "Mr. Kincaid says Folsum is a great place for kids."

Jim didn't look up. He had his baseball cap pulled low over his forehead, and his lanky body was slumped miserably in the seat.

He knew he was being very selfish but he couldn't help it. After all, it was asking a lot of a guy to give up everything.

His father had just received the job of a life-time—a post at Folsum National Laboratories in New Mexico. He had been handpicked by the company's president, Jefferson Kincaid, and would be making three times the salary he had earned back in California.

The problem was, Jim had to leave all his friends, and worst of all he had to give up his position as pitcher in his hometown summer league with a perfect no-loss record and only two games left to play.

"Don't worry about him, Mom." Laura, Jim's eight-year-old sister, scooted forward and whispered loudly to their mother in a teasing voice. "He's just having Heather Atkinson withdrawal." Laura fell back against the seat and covered her mouth to stifle her laughter.

Jim thought seriously about jerking one of Laura's long blond braids. But he didn't. The truth was he did miss Heather. She wasn't his girlfriend or anything, but who knew . . . if only they weren't moving.

He raised his cap a little and stared at his

father's back. Robert Stanton was a research scientist. He worked hard to support his family, and his big chance had finally come. The Wellington Foundation, along with Folsum Laboratories, had heard of the project Dr. Stanton had been working on dealing with a new plastic that could withstand tremendous heat.

The family would live in the small, elite community of Folsum, nestled at the base of New Mexico's Sacramento Mountains, while Dr. Stanton completed his research. Jim's mother had read Jim the brochures the company sent and had shown him the pictures of their new house. To her it was all incredible. For the first time in their lives they would be living in a really nice house in an equally nice neighborhood.

"Oh, look, Robert—there's the school."

Jim watched his mother grab his father's arm excitedly. She had gone on and on about the dumb school. It boasted the highest grade-point averages and the most distinguished alumni in the state, possibly the nation.

"Wait till they get ahold of the Ditz Brain," Jim mumbled just loud enough for his sister to hear.

She wrinkled her nose and stuck her tongue out at him. "You're the one who can't spell 'cat.' They probably won't even let you in the front door of the school." Laura folded her arms smugly.

Their father looked in the rearview mirror. "That'll be enough of that." He turned the corner and drove down a short street with houses on either side. He pulled the station wagon into the driveway of a large two-story brick house.

"You can get out now, kids. We're here."

CHAPTER 2

Jim slammed the car door. He had to admit, the house was impressive. The lawn was perfectly trimmed and the shrubs looked as if they had been manicured. Not one blade of grass was out of place. The other houses on the block looked almost exactly the same—except that they all had late-model cars sitting in their driveways.

"Must be a retirement community," Jim said. "I don't see any kids around."

His mother hugged him playfully. "Don't worry, kiddo. They'll probably be around later, after we've had time to unpack and get a few things in place."

"Everything's already in place." His father reached for a suitcase on top of the station wagon. "The company took care of it."

Jim's mother looked puzzled. "You mean they put away our dishes, clothes, and everything?"

"Mr. Kincaid said you'd be pleasantly surprised, Mary."

Mrs. Stanton frowned. "I don't know, Robert. How would they know where I wanted everything? I mean, really . . ."

Jim's father led the way to the front door and unlocked it. He pushed it open and let his family walk in first.

"Wow!" Laura skipped around the room. "Look at all the brand-new furniture."

Jim took his cap off and ran his hand through his hair. "You must have the wrong house, Dad. This isn't our stuff."

"It is now. The company took care of it. They put all our old things in storage." Dr. Stanton waved his hand. "All this is ours."

"Does that go for the kitchen too?" Mrs.

Stanton yelled from the next room. "All the dishes and pans are brand new."

Jim's father grinned. "Wait till you see the bedrooms."

Laura and Jim looked at each other and then raced up the stairs. Jim pushed open the first door on the left. He couldn't believe his eyes. Signed pictures of major-league baseball stars covered the walls. The furniture was dark oak. It all looked like something out of an expensive catalog. There were even clothes in the closets and drawers.

The walls of Laura's room were painted her favorite color—pink. Her bedroom set was white. In the center of the large canopy bed was a big, beautiful doll with long golden curls. Jim stood in the doorway and watched Laura timidly step toward the bed. She stopped and glanced back at him.

He rolled his eyes. "Pick it up, stupid. They put it there for you."

That was all she needed to hear. She ran to the bed and cradled the doll in her arms.

Jim walked back to his room and plopped down on the bed. He grudgingly looked around. The bedroom was twice as big as his old one.

His mother's voice interrupted his thoughts. "Jim! Laura! Come down here. We have visitors."

CHAPTER 3

Jim slid down the banister with Laura giggling and racing close behind him. When they reached the bottom they saw a woman and two kids, a boy about Jim's age and a little girl, standing stiffly in the living room and staring at them.

"This is Mrs. Tyler." Mrs. Stanton gestured toward the petite, well-dressed woman, who was holding a platter of cookies. "And these are her children, William and Karen."

"Please. Just call me Marcia," the woman said in a nervous, bubbly voice. She handed the platter to Mrs. Stanton. "These are for you. It's our way of saying welcome to the company."

The boy put his hand out to Jim. He smiled, but it was an odd smile, artificial and definitely not friendly. "We are very glad to have you here."

Jim shook the clammy hand and looked the boy up and down. He was wearing dress pants, a white starched shirt, and polished shoes. "Thanks, William. Hey, could you show me around town?"

The boy dropped Jim's hand and looked anxiously up at his mother. The woman put her arm around her son's shoulders. "I'm afraid not. Perhaps later . . . you know, when you've been here longer." She propelled the two children toward the door.

"Won't you stay and have a glass of iced tea or something?" Jim's mother asked.

The woman kept moving. "Thank you, no. We were instructed—that is, we were chosen —to welcome you and then let you get on with your day. It was so nice to meet you all. Goodbye!" She pulled the door shut behind her.

Jim's father raised one eyebrow. "Strange woman."

"She might be strange, but boy, can she cook! Taste one of these." Laura held up one of the small white cookies. It had a perfect red rosette in the center.

"Be careful, Laura, they probably have some kind of poison in them." Jim sat down on the arm of the new couch. "I hope everybody in this town isn't as weird as they are." He leaned back and sighed. "Did you see how that William was dressed, and what happened when I asked him to show me around?"

Jim's father hesitated, thinking; then he shrugged. "Why don't you go out and see the neighborhood for yourself? Your mom and I have a couple of things to catch up on here anyway. Take Laura and be back by supper."

Jim thought about asking if he could leave Laura behind, but the look on his father's face already told him the answer.

"Okay. Come on, squirt. Let's go exploring and see what kind of mess we've gotten ourselves into."

Laura followed him through the door and

down the sidewalk. "Look, Jim. There's some-body." She pointed at the mailman, who was carefully sorting through the letters he held as he walked toward them.

The short, balding man stopped in front of them. "I'd say you two are new around here."

Jim nodded. "How did you know?"

The man looked nervously behind him. "When you've been with the company a while you . . . well, let's just say that you don't quite fit the mold . . . yet."

The man looked around again and then moved past them. Over his shoulder he said in a loud voice, "So nice to have you here."

"Everyone keeps saying that," Laura said.

"I know," Jim said, and started walking. "But somehow I get the feeling they don't really mean it."

They walked until they reached downtown Folsum. Each neighborhood they passed through looked exactly like theirs.

"I don't know who designed this town, but they sure didn't have much of an imagina-tion." Jim looked at his watch. "We have just enough time to get a look at Main Street and maybe play a fast video game before we have to head back."

Laura pulled on the back of his T-shirt. "Jimmy, I don't like this place. Where are all the people?"

Jim shrugged and looked at the deserted sidewalks. "Maybe we've moved into a town full of blood-sucking zombies that only come out at midnight."

Laura stopped. "That's not funny. I want to go home."

"I'm only kidding, squirt. Look, there are people in that grocery store across the street."

They watched a woman who could have been Mrs. Tyler's twin sister, except that she was taller and had darker hair, come out of the store and put a sack of groceries in her car. A little girl dressed in a white pinafore almost identical to Karen Tyler's followed her.

Jim raised one eyebrow. "Must be a shortage of clothes stores." He felt another tug on the back of his shirt. "What is it now?"

Laura pointed to a sign in the window of a

small ice cream shop. "Can we go in?" She looked at him hopefully.

"Normally I'd say forget it. But since I don't see an arcade, it looks like ice cream is the only thing this town has going for it."

Jim pushed the door open and a little bell jingled from above. They sat down at the counter and waited. Finally a man dressed in white came in from one of the back rooms.

The man's eyes narrowed when he saw them. "You two aren't from the mountains, are you?"

Jim shook his head. "We're the Stantons. We just moved in today. My dad's a scientist."

"Oh." The man's face changed. He smiled the same sort of strange smile William had given them earlier. "That's different, then. What can I get for you?"

They placed their orders and sat on the stools, silently eating. No other customers came in. Jim noticed that the waiter never moved very far away, almost as if he was keeping an eye on them.

When they finished, Jim stepped up to the cash register to pay. Before he could get his money out, the man held his hand up. "It's on the house, son."

Jim looked confused. "Thanks, mister."

The man gave him the strange smile again. "No problem. Welcome to the company."

CHAPTER 4

"Don't worry, Mom. I'll be careful."

Mrs. Stanton poured a glass of orange juice and pushed it across the counter. "We've only been here a couple of days and you don't know your way around yet."

Jim took a gulp of the juice and started for the front door. "I'm only going for a short hike in the mountains. Besides, how am I ever going to know where anything is if I don't get out there and find out?"

"All right, but just be sure you're back here

by two o'clock. We have to go down to the lab for our physicals."

Jim set the glass down. "The whole family has to have physicals?"

His mother nodded. "Something to do with the company insurance policy."

"Why can't you just give them my last report? It's only three months old."

"I already thought of that, but your dad says the company insists on giving its own."

"I guess it won't kill me." He grabbed a left-over cookie and headed out the door. "See you later."

He stopped on the front step and looked around. As usual, there were no people in sight, but he thought he saw a curtain move on the second floor of the last house on the block. He stared at the window a moment, then shrugged and started up into the hills.

The woods were thick with brush. Sometimes he had to break off branches to get through. The trees were still green and beautiful, even though summer was drawing to a close.

Jim thought of his friends back home and how different it was going to be to start school without them this year. He shook the thought from his mind. It felt good to get outside the town. Folsum was stuffy and there wasn't anything to do. No mall or arcade. They didn't even have a ball field.

He walked aimlessly for almost a mile until he came to a meadow. Off to one side of the clearing was a small, dark pond.

"All right!" Jim said out loud. "Things are starting to look up."

He raced to the edge of the water and skipped a rock halfway across the surface. He picked up another rock and pretended to be an announcer.

"And here is the world-famous White Sox pitcher, Strikeout King Jim Stanton, stepping up to the mound."

He reared back to wind up for the pitch.

Before he could let it go, another rock came sailing out of the woods behind him and skipped the entire length of the pond.

Jim whipped around. "Who's there?"

There was no answer.

He scanned the trees, but no one was in sight. Quietly he stepped away from the pond into the cover of the forest and listened.

An eerie screeching echoed across the meadow. Then nothing.

A lump caught in his throat. Aloud, in case anyone happened to be listening, he said, "Wouldn't you know it. The only halfway decent place to go around here and it's haunted." He walked cautiously back to the pond and looked down at the water.

He stared at his unhappy reflection and sighed. "It's probably time for me to get back to Weirdsville anyway."

Another reflection appeared in the water beside his. It was the face of a dark-haired girl about his age.

His eyes widened. He thought about running but his legs were frozen and wouldn't cooperate.

The face smiled. "Hi, Strikeout King Jim Stanton. My name's Maria."

Jim looked up. Hanging in a tree above the pond was a girl. A real live human girl with a small brown monkey clinging to her back.

He breathed a sigh of relief. "You had me scared there for a minute. I thought you were a . . . well, a . . ."

"A ghost?" The girl slid back on the branch and dropped lightly to the ground. She pushed a strand of her long, thick hair behind one ear. "I know. I planned it that way." She held the monkey in her arms. "Sammy and I had to see if you were one of them."

"One of them?"

Maria nodded. "You know, one of the mad scientists from down below. Sammy came from down there. My uncle rescued him from one of their crazy experiments."

Jim's chin went out. "My dad is a scientist."

Maria let Sammy slip to the ground and walked around him. "I don't get it. How'd they miss you?"

Jim closed his eyes in exasperation. "Is everybody in this part of the world crazy? What are you talking about?"

She folded her arms and continued to study him. "My uncle says it's the water, but I think they do brain removal. Which is it?"

Jim threw up his hands. "I give up. The first

person I run across who will actually talk to me is a complete wacko and carries a monkey around on her back." He turned and stalked off in the direction of town.

"Wait!" Maria ran after him.

Jim stopped and turned around. "What?"

"You wouldn't want to play catch, would you, Jim Stanton?"

"Did you say catch, like in baseball?"

Maria nodded. "That is, if you scientist types aren't too wimpy to throw a ball."

Jim smiled in spite of himself. "You just lead the way."

CHAPTER 5

Maria led him over the next ridge and down into a lush green valley. A weathered log cabin with a rickety old truck parked in front of it sat in the shadows of the tall pine trees.

As they approached the house, Maria called out, "It's me, Uncle Max. I brought a friend."

She whispered to Jim, "You have to do that. He doesn't see so good anymore and he's liable to shoot first and ask questions later."

Jim stared at her. "You're kidding, right?"

Maria didn't answer.

A gruff voice boomed at them. "Who's that with you?"

Maria glanced at Jim with a twinkle in her eye. "I found a flatlander down by the pond."

"What?" the voice barked. A big man with a scraggly gray beard limped out onto the wooden porch. He leaned on a gnarled walking stick. "You know better than to bring his kind up here. You're just asking for trouble."

Maria let Sammy go and stepped up on the porch beside her uncle. "He's new down there. They haven't had time to work on him yet. Besides, I'm bored and he says he can catch."

The elderly man's lip curled. He snarled down at Jim. "What are you doing up here? Snooping?"

Jim shook his head. "I didn't even know anybody lived up here."

"Well, they do." The man's face softened slightly. He turned to Maria. "Don't keep him up here too long." He inclined his head in the direction of Folsum. "No telling what they might do to him if they found out."

The big man turned and slowly limped back into the cabin, shaking his head. "Too bad."

Jim frowned. "What's he talking about? Who's going to do something to me?"

Maria jumped off the porch and sat on the edge, stroking Sammy under the chin. "It's probably better if you don't know. After all, you *are* going to have to live down there."

"Look," Jim snapped. "I'm getting sick and tired of all this mysterious mumbo jumbo. If you know something, spit it out. If you don't, then shut up about it."

Sammy didn't like his tone of voice and started chattering loudly.

Maria hesitated. She stroked Sammy again and then put him inside the screen door.

"All right, I'll tell you. Ten years ago my uncle Max used to work at Folsum Laboratories as a custodian. He loved his job. . . . Of course, most of the people were different back then."

Jim kicked at a rock. "Did he get fired?"

"In a way. He was asked to resign."

"Why?"

"One day when he was cleaning Kincaid's

24

office—Kincaid's the president—he came across some documents on a top-secret experiment. The company was doing high-level radiation experiments on people without their knowledge."

"Did he go to the cops?"

"He tried. He made copies of the information and called the authorities. But before he could prove anything, his house was ransacked and the papers were stolen. The thieves beat him up and broke one of his legs. The next day Kincaid asked him to resign."

"Man, those guys don't fool around." Jim scratched his head. "What makes you think they might try to do something to me? After all, that was a long time ago and they probably don't do stuff like that anymore. Besides, my dad's a scientist. It would be pretty tough to get anything past him."

Maria stood up and brushed the dirt off her jeans. "Haven't you noticed that the people down there act a little strange?"

"Yeah." Jim smiled. "If I had to guess, I'd say the laboratory's been turning out a bunch of zombies."

Maria didn't laugh. "You might think it's funny, but don't say I didn't try to warn you."

"Okay, you warned me. I'll keep an eye out for people who glow in the dark and anyone who goes by the name of Dr. Frankenstein." He looked at his watch. "I thought we were going to play some catch."

Maria reached under the porch and brought out two gloves and a ball. She tossed him one of the gloves. Before he had time to get it all the way onto his hand, she burned the ball into his stomach.

He doubled over. "Hey! What was that for?"

She glared at him. "Better learn to think fast, Young Frankenstein."

CHAPTER 6

Jim smiled to himself as he made his way back down the mountainside. Maria was actually a pretty good ballplayer. She was, that is, after she got over being mad at him.

Things were definitely looking up. He'd found a pond and a new friend all in one day. Maria had invited him to come back the next day. She said she would show him a cave in a hill behind her house where prospectors used to mine gold. The tunnels stretched for miles. She said there was one that went almost all the way to Folsum.

When he reached the edge of town, he hesitated. Although he hadn't admitted it to Maria, something about Folsum really did bother him.

That something, a feeling that perhaps someone was watching, made him decide to find a different route to his house. Staying low behind the tall redwood fences of his neighbors' backyards, he worked his way along the alley. He let himself through the backyard gate and entered the house by the back door.

His mother and father were having a discussion in the hall. "Just the man I need to talk to." Dr. Stanton motioned for Jim to come closer. "I hear you were off up in the woods today?"

Jim nodded. He started to tell them about Maria and the pond and everything, but his father cut him off.

"I know you're bored, Jim, but you can't go up in the mountains anymore. Kincaid called me into his office and asked me to tell you."

"Wait a minute." Jim's eyes narrowed. He remembered the moving curtain earlier in the day. "How did Kincaid know I was taking a hike today?"

His father shook his head. "I really don't know, son. But I do know that it's against company policy to let our children traipse around in the woods by themselves. Kincaid said there were undesirables living up there and that we should be extremely careful."

"But Dad, I—"

Robert Stanton held up his hand. "End of discussion. We're new here and I'm sure Mr. Kincaid knows the area better than we do." He reached for his briefcase. "It's time for us to go down to the lab. Where's Laura?"

Jim didn't answer. A hundred thoughts were racing through his mind. *Who is this Kincaid, and why does he want to keep people away from the woods? What is he afraid of?*

Mrs. Stanton had gathered up Laura and her doll and was waiting for Jim by the door. "Dad's already in the car, Jim. Get a move on. He doesn't want you to make a bad impression on his boss."

"Right." Jim mumbled under his breath. "We can't have the great Mr. Kincaid thinking we're part of the 'undesirable' crowd now, can we?"

"What was that, son?" Mrs. Stanton asked.

Jim held the door for her. "Oh, nothing, Mom. I was just saying how much I was looking forward to meeting Dad's boss."

CHAPTER 7

An electric eye scanned the identification card Dr. Stanton held out the car window. The gates opened and a robotlike voice told them to drive ahead. Jim watched the two security guards march back and forth on the catwalk above their heads. The compound was entirely surrounded by an eight-foot fence that was topped with barbed wire, similar to fences on military bases.

Dr. Stanton stopped the station wagon in front of a long white building with a sign across the front that said FOLSOM NATIONAL LABORATORIES—JEFFERSON KINCAID, PRESIDENT.

Jim's parents were jabbering away about what a wonderful facility it was and how lucky Dr. Stanton was to be working here, but Jim wasn't paying any attention. Now more than ever he was convinced that something odd was going on in Folsum and that it was about to involve his family in some way.

He tried to take mental notes on everything as they walked down the hall, attempting to find anything that seemed out of place. His father explained that the area they were in was the lab's own private medical complex. The business offices were at the other end of the wing, and the experiments took place in various secure, specially built laboratories.

A tall, distinguished-looking man with gray sideburns and bushy black eyebrows was waiting for them at the reception desk. He spoke to Jim's father. "Nice-looking family, Stanton. Just the kind we like here at Folsum."

"Thank you, sir."

The man didn't wait to be introduced. "I'm Jefferson Kincaid." He eyed Jim for a moment. "You must be the ballplayer."

Jim nodded.

"It's good to have hobbies, as long as they don't interfere with responsibilities."

"It's not a hobby with me, sir. I intend to make it my career."

The man's cold blue eyes flashed. "I suppose we'll see about that, won't we?"

A woman in a long white coat walked up to them. She looked at her clipboard and asked them to follow her to a small waiting room.

"It was nice meeting your family, Stanton." Kincaid put his hands in the pockets of his lab coat, smiling slightly. "It might be wise to keep an eye on the ballplayer, though. Looks like he could be a handful."

Jim felt the man's eyes on his back as they walked down the hall. He was glad when they turned the corner and went into the waiting room.

It wasn't his first time inside a laboratory. He'd been in the one where his father used to work several times. On the surface things looked about the same here. People scurried around in lab coats, carrying important-looking papers.

But there was one vast difference.

Silence.

None of the employees spoke to the others. They didn't nod or acknowledge each other in any way. It was as if each one were a robot in his or her own little world.

Suddenly the quiet was broken.

"Stanton, Robert."

Jim jumped. A burly man in a white uniform stood in the doorway. Jim's father laughed. "Relax, son. It's not the end of the world, it's only a physical."

Jim didn't smile.

The man came back twice more, once for Mrs. Stanton and then again for Laura.

Jim waited more than an hour.

Finally a small, elderly gentleman appeared in the doorway. "Are you Jim Stanton?"

Jim nodded.

"You're the last one, then. They've had a slight emergency and they asked me to finish you up. I'm Dr. Wiley."

The doctor led him down a long corridor, mumbling to himself all the way. "I can do this. They say I'm too old and that my mind is failing. But they're wrong. You can see that, can't you?" He opened the door to an examining room without waiting for an answer. "Crawl up on the table, young man, and we'll get this over with."

The elderly man tapped Jim's knee and watched his reflexes over the top of his glasses. "You look pretty healthy."

"I am."

"Good, then we'll skip right to the blood test." The doctor went to a table and fiddled with a long syringe. He dropped something on the floor that resembled a small black dot. He cursed and reached to pick it up. "Oh, I hope it's not damaged."

As he stood up, he noticed that Jim was watching. His eyes grew wide. "Please, if you should remember, don't mention seeing this to anyone. They're already talking about replacing me."

The doctor turned back to the table and brought the needle up next to Jim's arm. Before Jim could protest, the little man jabbed the wide tip into his arm and pushed something under his skin.

"Wait a minute!" Jim grabbed at the syringe and jerked it out of his arm. "What do you think you're doing? You're not taking blood."

The doctor stepped back, clasped his hands in front of him, and quietly observed his patient.

Jim tried to stand up. The room was whirling around him. He let go of the table and tried to take a step.

The floor was coming closer.

Suddenly everything went black.

CHAPTER 8

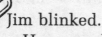

Jim blinked.

He opened his eyes to a blurry world. A few things gradually started coming into focus. There were pictures of baseball stars on the wall. He was home, in his own bed.

Something was wrong. He tried desperately to remember. His head was pounding. What was it?

The door opened and his mother and father came into the room. His mother was carrying a tray with a glass of juice on it. "How are you feeling, James?" She sat on the edge of the bed and propped up his pillow.

He stared at her. It was his mother, all right, but she was different. She was dressed in a crisp tailored suit instead of jeans, and she had called him James. She had never called him James before.

Jim rubbed his head. "What happened?"

His father eyed him coldly. "You had an accident. Apparently you took a walk in the woods and had a nasty fall. We rushed you to the emergency room, but they said it was nothing serious. You'll be fine with a little rest."

"The woods?" Jim's forehead wrinkled. "I don't remember falling."

"Dr. Wiley said you might not remember a few things for a while, dear." His mother folded back the top of his bedspread and stood up. "Don't worry about it. Just rest."

Jim's father gave him a mechanical smile. "Your mother and I are on our way to attend a company meeting. We should be back in about an hour. If you need anything, tell Laura to give us a call. The number is by the downstairs telephone."

They left the room, and Jim felt more mixed up than ever. He couldn't remember even being in the woods. But there was something familiar about the name Wiley. The more he thought about it the more his head ached.

He tried to sit up. His head thundered with pain. "Lau-ra!"

Laura skipped into his room, carrying her new doll. "Do you need something? Mother and Father said to assist you any way I could."

Jim studied her. Even Laura was different. She was dressed in an Alice-in-Wonderland type of dress. He shook his head. It only made the pain worse.

"I need a painkiller, Laura. Go downstairs and see if there's some aspirin or something in the cabinet."

"No. I was told not to give you drugs. I must obey."

"What?"

"I must obey. However, I am allowed to read you a story and to keep you company. What would you like to hear?"

Jim grabbed his throbbing head with both hands. "The sound of you leaving my room. If you're not going to help me, then just go away."

Without a word Laura turned and left the room.

Jim slowly stood. He inched his way along the bed to the wall and leaned against it for a full minute. As long as he didn't try to think, his head didn't pound so hard.

He decided not to try the stairs. Instead he made his way into his parents' bathroom and found a bottle of aspirin in the medicine cabinet. After he had swallowed a couple, he sat down to rest on the edge of their bed.

The telephone rang.

Jim scooted along the side of the bed and picked it up. "Hello?"

"Hi, Jim. It's me, Maria."

"Maria?"

She laughed. "How quickly they forget. You know, Maria from the pond."

"Pond?" Jim felt like an idiot. He couldn't remember anyone named Maria.

There was a moment of silence on the other end. "Jim, are you okay?"

"No. No, I'm not. My head feels like a freight train ran over it. I'm sorry, I don't seem to remember you."

A woman's voice came on the wire. "This line is temporarily out of order."

The phone went dead.

"Hello?" There was no answer, and Jim put the receiver down.

He fell back on the pillows. What was going on? Why couldn't he remember things? And why was everybody in his family acting so weird?

It wasn't just his head that hurt. There was a burning sensation rippling up and down his arm. A square white bandage was taped to the top of the arm near his shoulder. He peeled it back to get a better look.

Underneath was a small red lump.

"Insect bite."

Jim looked up. Laura was standing in the doorway, watching him. "Mother and Father said to tell you it was an insect bite."

"What do you mean, they said to tell me?"

Laura didn't answer. Instead she darted off down the hall to her room.

Jim managed to get to his feet. "Laura, come back here. Laura!"

The pain increased. The room was spinning out of control.

"Oh no." He tried to make it to the wall. "Not again . . ."

CHAPTER 9

It was better, easier, not to think, not to question.

Jim sat on the back porch and watched the moon slowly climb over the top of the mountains. It had been three days since his accident and he still hadn't remembered anything.

His family had done their best to assure him that everything was fine. But deep down he knew it wasn't. How could he recall the tiniest things about his early family life, things like meals he'd eaten and birthday presents he'd received, and yet have blocked out everything else concerning his past? Every time he asked a question or made an attempt to remember, an excruciating pain vibrated through his head.

A new car had been delivered to their house. It was almost identical to the other expensive cars up and down the block. Jim was told it was company policy. They wanted to keep their workers happy.

His mother and father seemed to love their new life here. Every night, like clockwork, they attended company meetings, and when they came home they acted even more like strangers than before.

Laura kept to herself. She never played outside or asked him to take her anywhere. She just wanted to be left alone.

"Pssst."

Jim sat up. The noise was coming from behind the tall redwood fence surrounding their backyard.

"Pssst. Jim, over here."

Jim moved to the fence and looked over. A pretty girl with long dark hair was standing on the other side.

"Who are you?"

She held her finger to her lips. "Quiet, you big lunkhead. Do you want them to find me?"

"That depends. Who are you hiding from?"

A small brown monkey climbed up the girl's back and jumped over the fence.

"Sammy, get back here," she whispered. "You're going to ruin everything."

Jim's head started to pound. He was sure he knew that monkey, and he'd seen the girl somewhere before too. The name "Maria" sprang to his mind. He said it out loud. "Maria?"

She put her hands on her hips. "So you remember my name. Well that's a start at least." She stepped inside the gate, scooped Sammy up in her arms, and held the gate open. "Come on. We don't have much time."

Bewilderment clouded Jim's aching brain. "Where are we going?"

"I'm taking you to my uncle Max. He's going to try to help you."

Help. He definitely needed help. It hurt too much to ask any more questions. He walked out the gate and followed her up into the mountains.

CHAPTER 10

The girl knew where she was going. And somehow it seemed right to follow her. She was holding his hand, leading him rapidly through a pitch-black tunnel with only a small flashlight. He tripped once and fell to his knees. She stopped and pointed the light so that he could see. He'd tripped over an old, dusty crate labeled DYNAMITE.

At the end of the tunnel, they climbed out of a small, cavelike entrance into the bright moonlight. A few feet in front of them was the back of an old log cabin.

The girl called out softly, "I'm back, Uncle Max, and I brought him with me."

The heavy wooden door squeaked open. A gravelly voice said, "Hurry, Maria. You don't understand the chance we're taking."

Maria grabbed Jim's hand tightly and pulled him along as she ran to the cabin. Once inside, she sat the monkey on a bed, bolted the door, and began covering the windows with blankets.

Jim plopped down beside the monkey. He still didn't understand any of this. All he knew was that his head was pounding furiously and if these people could do anything to help him, he was more than ready for it.

The grizzled old man moved beside him. "How did they do it, son?"

Jim stared at him. He wasn't in the mood for games. He probably shouldn't even be here. His parents would be worried. On second thought, nothing much seemed to worry them lately.

The girl walked over. "He says his head hurts and he doesn't seem to be able to remember much."

The big man sighed. "You're going to have to try to think, son. Did they give you something? Did you have an operation of some kind?"

Jim held his head. He felt like screaming. In as calm a voice as he could manage, he said, "That's just it. I can't think. Every time I try, it feels like my head will burst into a million pieces." Frustrated, he scratched at the bandage on his arm.

"What's that?" Maria asked.

Jim pulled up his shirtsleeve. "I guess it's a bug bite. It itches like fire."

The old man gently rolled back the gauze wrapping. "That's it. Maria, we'll need some boiling water and my sharpest hunting knife."

"Hold on." Jim tried to protest, to fight, but he was too weak.

The big man took a large brown bottle off a shelf and poured some of the contents on a red cloth. He helped Jim lie back on the bed.

Jim saw the cloth coming at his face. Felt it

cover his nostrils. He tried to turn his head away but it was no use.

Max held on to him and spoke in a soothing tone. "Now you just relax, son. If my guess is right, we'll have you feeling like a brand-new lad in about ten minutes."

CHAPTER 11

Jim was dreaming. He was back at the lab clinic. Everything was black. He couldn't see a thing, but he could hear voices.

"Wiley, you bumbling old coot. You gave the boy the wrong implant. That one is still in the early experimental stage. We should have done away with you years ago."

The older doctor's voice shook with fear. "I'm sorry, Ryan. Please don't terminate me. I'll take it out and do it over."

"Wait!" a familiar voice said. It was Kincaid. "This could actually prove useful to us.

We'll let the boy carry the G-2 implant for a few days and then bring him in for questioning. Who knows what sort of guinea pig he'll make?"

"But what about his family? They received the mind-control device. Won't the boy notice that things are different at home?" asked the man called Ryan.

"Don't question my orders," Kincaid snarled. Then he chuckled wickedly. "If the implant works correctly, our little ballplayer will be in terrible agony every time he uses his brain. After a while he won't even know his own name."

"Jim."

A younger, softer voice was calling to him.

"Wake up, Strikeout King. You're talking in your sleep."

Jim's eyes flew open. Maria was sitting on the edge of the bed. "It's about time you came back. I was starting to get worried," she said.

Jim sat up and grabbed her roughly by the shoulders. "I remember, Maria. I remember everything. We have to call the police. Kincaid is after my family."

"Calm down, boy." Maria's uncle Max stepped up beside them. "How are you feeling after our makeshift surgery?"

"Surgery?"

Max held up a jar with a tiny black spot rolling around in it. He pointed at the new bandage on Jim's arm. "We took this little beggar out of your shoulder. Apparently it was causing all the trouble."

"All right!" Jim shouted. "That's even better; now we have solid evidence. Kincaid will never see daylight again."

"I'm afraid it's not that easy." Max set the jar on the shelf. "Remember what happened to me?" He looked down at his twisted leg. "We're going to have to take this thing slow and make sure we have all the cards in our favor before we tip our hand."

"Uncle Max is right, Jim. While you were out we talked it over. You have to go back and pretend that nothing happened."

"Are you serious? My whole family is under that goon's control."

"They'll be fine," Maria said. "Kincaid doesn't seem to want to hurt them. We have to have more time to collect concrete evidence, more documentation on his plans, enough so that there won't be any question about his guilt."

Max helped Jim to his feet. "It's the only way, son, believe me. Maria's going to take you back through the mine shaft now. Hopefully no one has missed you. Remember to put on a good act for everyone, including your family . . . and look for any opportunities to discover more proof."

Jim leaned against the wall. "Why is Kincaid doing this? Why is he after us?"

"It's not just your family." Max led him to the door. "Kincaid has the whole town under his thumb. We don't know any of the details, but with your help, maybe we can find out what's going on."

Jim was reluctant to go. "How can I contact you? I'm pretty sure they have the phone lines tapped."

"Leave a message at the entrance to the tunnel. Maria will show you where. You'd better go before they realize you're missing. Those people don't take interference lightly."

CHAPTER 12

Maria moved the branches covering the end of the tunnel and spoke in a low voice. "It looks like you're clear back to your gate." She turned to face him in the moonlight. "Be careful. If things start to go wrong, get out. We can always come back for your family later."

Jim squeezed her hand. "Thanks for everything, Maria. No matter how this turns out, I want you and your uncle to know that I really appreciate what you've done."

Maria held on to his hand for a second

more, then let go. "You'd better hurry. Don't forget, I'll be checking for your messages."

"I won't forget." Jim arranged the brush in front of the opening. He crouched low and started down the hill toward his house.

The lights were all out inside the houses on his block. He'd been right about his parents' being unconcerned. They had gone to sleep hours before and had assumed that he had done the same.

Morning came way too early for Jim. It had been days since he'd really slept, and now that was all his worn-out body wanted to do. He had to force himself out of bed so that no one would be suspicious.

He'd barely made it to a sitting position when the door opened. It was his mother, immaculately dressed, with a fake Kewpie-doll smile on her face.

"And how are we doing today, James?"

Showtime, Jim realized. He contorted his face and glared at her through half-closed lids. "My head is killing me."

She patted his hair. It reminded him of the way he'd seen her pet his aunt Trudy's temperamental poodle.

"We're going to take care of that today, dear. President Kincaid wants to see you down at the laboratory this afternoon at one o'clock. He thinks he might be able to help you. Won't that be nice?"

Jim's mind raced. He had to get a message to Maria.

"In the meantime, dear," his mother went on, "I have to go out. Laura has been instructed to stay with you."

"I don't need Laura. I'll be fine by myself."

Mrs. Stanton's face went blank. "Laura has been instructed to stay with you." She turned on her heel and left the room.

"Great," Jim groaned. He reached for his clothes.

There was a knock on the door. "Are you dressed? It's me, Laura. I'm supposed to keep you company this morning."

Jim pulled his T-shirt on over his head. "No, I'm not dressed. I'll let you know when

I'm through." He slid into his jeans, laced up his high-tops, and tiptoed to the window. His room was on the second floor, but if he tied his sheets together—

"I thought you said you weren't dressed!" Laura stood in the doorway, staring at him accusingly.

"I wasn't. Besides, who invited you in here, squirt? Get lost."

"I cannot."

Jim studied his sister. An idea popped into his head. "Laura, who do you have to obey?"

"My elders. I must obey my elders."

"What happens if you don't?"

"Punishment."

"How old are you, Laura?"

"Eight."

"And how old am I?"

"Thirteen."

"So I guess that makes me your elder, doesn't it?"

Laura looked scared and confused. "I must obey my elders."

Here goes nothing, Jim thought. "Laura, I'm

your elder and I'm ordering you to stand in that corner." He pointed to the one by his closet.

She didn't question him. Before he could blink she was standing in the corner.

Jim grabbed a notepad and a pencil from his desk.

They're taking me to Kincaid at one o'clock. I'll try to get the goods on him. If you don't hear from me again, call the cops.

He ripped off the sheet of paper and stuffed it in his pocket. Laura was still standing rigidly in the corner. A pang of guilt tweaked his conscience.

Don't worry, squirt. I promise I'll be right back.

CHAPTER 13

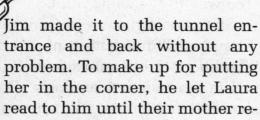

Jim made it to the tunnel entrance and back without any problem. To make up for putting her in the corner, he let Laura read to him until their mother returned from her meeting.

She found them on the back porch. Her high heels clicked on the cement. "Come, James, it's time to go."

"Go where?" Jim held his head and pretended to be in agony.

"Don't you remember? President Kincaid would like to see you."

He stood and followed her through the house. "How am I supposed to remember anything with this king-sized headache?"

The new car had leather upholstery. It smelled as if it was fresh off the showroom floor. Mrs. Stanton backed it out of the driveway and drove toward the laboratory.

Jim rested his head against the window and watched his mother out of the corner of his eye. Her expression was blank. Nothing seemed to register. She didn't say a word all the way to the compound.

She parked the car in front of the business complex. "President Kincaid said that you should go in by yourself, James."

Jim opened the car door. He stopped and leaned close to her. "When this is all over, I hope you'll be proud of me, Mom."

A tiny flicker of emotion flashed in her eyes and was gone. "Goodbye, James."

He sighed, said goodbye, stepped out of the car, and watched her drive away.

It was time. He turned to face the tall, white building looming in front of him. The glass doors slid open and a big man with beady black eyes walked up to him.

"You must be Jim Stanton. I'm Dr. Ryan, President Kincaid's personal assistant. He asked me to escort you to his office."

Ryan! Jim swallowed hard. That was the name of the third doctor who knew about his implant. *Keep cool,* he reminded himself. *Everything rides on your performance.*

He screwed up his face and tried his best to look as if he were suffering. "I sure hope you guys can help me, Doctor. I'm in a whole lot of pain here."

"You've come to the right place, Jim. Follow me."

Dr. Ryan led him down the hall to an oak door with PRESIDENT KINCAID engraved on a gold plaque. "Go on in, Jim. Make yourself comfortable. The president will be with you in about ten minutes. He's just finishing up a meeting."

Dr. Ryan closed the door and left Jim standing in a plush office. Thick white carpet covered the floor, and an oversized mahogany desk sat in front of the window. Overstuffed chairs and a couch were arranged in front of the desk. A tall filing cabinet stood near the end of the couch.

Jim glanced back at the door and then went to work. There were only ten short minutes for him to find something. He tried the filing cabinet. It was locked. Frantically he searched the top drawer of the desk. Miraculously, a tiny gold key was taped to the inside front of the drawer.

It fit the lock of the filing cabinet.

He thumbed through the files. A large folder marked PROJECT: A PERFECT WORLD caught his eye. Quickly he pulled it out and scanned it. It was a report on mind control done by Jefferson Kincaid, containing the names of every person in Folsum who had been used in his project. There was also a binder outlining Kincaid's plans to set himself up as the dictator of a new country.

"This guy's nuts," Jim mumbled.

There was a tap on the window. Jim jumped and nearly dropped the file.

It was Maria. Sammy's head was poking out

of a blue bag she carried on her shoulder. She held up a pair of bolt cutters and smiled. "I cut a hole in the back fence."

Jim pushed open the window and helped Maria inside.

He showed her the folder. "I've got it, Maria."

"I hate to burst your bubble, Jim Stanton. But I'm afraid you'll have to give that back."

Jim whirled around. President Kincaid was watching him with an amused look on his face. Dr. Ryan moved to the file, jerked it out of the boy's hands, and handed it to Kincaid.

"I was hoping you were smarter, Jim." Kincaid laughed and pointed to a surveillance camera near the door. "We've been watching you."

"Let go of me, you big goons!" Maria yelled.

Two men in white coats dropped the struggling Maria in a heap on the floor. Sammy clung to her neck and chattered angrily. She quickly scrambled to her feet, adjusted the strap on her bag, and tried to bluff. "You'd better have a good explanation for this, Kincaid."

"Oh, I do, my dear." The president winked at her and clapped his hands. "This is wonderful. I was wondering how I could manage to get both of you, and you made it so easy for me. How considerate."

Kincaid looked past Maria to the two aides. "You did an excellent job. Wait for me down the hall while I have a chat with our little friends here."

"What are you talking about?" Maria said, fuming.

Kincaid waited until the aides left the room before he continued. "The operator traced your call. That's how we knew you had been in contact with young Jim. Then when William Tyler reported that Jim had left his house again this morning—"

"So that's how you knew I was up in the mountains that day. That turkey down the street has been watching me."

Kincaid nodded. "He's quite effective, really. Completely loyal."

"Right," Jim said, smirking. "As long as he's wearing your mind-control device."

Kincaid sat on the edge of his desk. "I suppose it serves no purpose to tell you this, since you won't remember anything when Ryan is through with both of you. But I am extremely proud of our little project, so let me explain it to you."

He straightened the file and laid it on top of his desk. "You see, I have perfected the ultimate in mind control. No one in history has ever gotten this far. Oh, we've tried other drugs, even done a few lobotomies. But this . . . this is perfection. Once a person receives the implant, he is given certain suggestions at our little company meetings, and then he becomes a completely happy and fulfilled worker. It has worldwide implications. Crime can become nonexistent, productivity can be increased by fifty percent, and we may actually achieve world peace in our lifetime. Imagine."

Jim looked at him in disgust. "You don't want world peace. You want to be some kind of new Hitler and rule the world."

"Who better?" Kincaid stood up. "Today, Folsum." An evil smile contorted his face. "Tomorrow, the world. Now, as much as I've enjoyed chatting with you, I have other things to attend to." He stepped to the door and looked back at Dr. Ryan. "Take them to the medical wing, and this time make sure they no longer pose any kind of threat." The door closed with a thud.

"My pleasure." Ryan reached for Maria.

Sammy screeched, leaped for the man's face, and hung on.

"Get it off!" Ryan fell to the floor, struggling to pry the snarling, hissing monkey off his face.

"Now's our chance, Maria!" Jim grabbed the file and slipped out the narrow window. "Come on. What are you waiting for?"

Maria looked back at Sammy. She bit her lip and then dived for the window.

CHAPTER 14

They crossed the compound and raced to the hole Maria had cut in the fence. Time was running out. It would be only seconds before Kincaid was after them.

Sammy had jumped out the window after them, and was now perched safely on Maria's shoulder. A siren went off, and behind them they heard people yelling and dogs barking. Jim pulled Maria behind a supply shed.

"We're not going to make it very far this way. They'll have us before we reach the tunnel. Our only hope is to split up." He handed her the file. "You go for help and I'll stay here and keep them busy."

Maria didn't argue. She slid the blue bag she had been carrying off her shoulder. "Here. This might come in handy." Without another word she turned and headed for the fence.

Jim unzipped the bag. Maria had come prepared for a war. There were matches and several sticks of dynamite from the tunnel. There was also a familiar-looking brown bottle. It was the ether Max had used to knock Jim out when Max had removed the implant.

The yelling and the barking were getting louder. They were coming fast. He had to buy Maria some time.

Jim reached for one of the sticks of dynamite, lit it, and placed it next to the shed. Then he ran as fast as he could toward the next building.

The first explosion cracked the air with a satisfying roar. But seconds later, whatever was stored in the building caught fire and mushroomed into a giant burning cloud that made Jim feel as if he were in the middle of a firestorm.

More sirens went off, and people started streaming out of the buildings. Jim watched from around the corner. Security guards and dogs were still looking for them. He lit another stick of dynamite and threw it into the parking lot under one of the new cars.

He didn't wait around to watch it blow. Instead he ran the length of the building and looked for his next target.

Dr. Ryan, scratched and bleeding, was standing on the steps of the business office.

Jim pulled off his T-shirt and soaked it with the ether. He held it behind his back and called to the doctor. "Looking for me, barf-face?"

Dr. Ryan snorted and charged for him. Jim stayed where he was until the big man was on him. Just as a huge arm reached for him, Jim stuffed the shirt into the man's battered face and hung on. For a second Dr. Ryan struggled; then he fell limp to the ground.

The strong odor of the ether began to overpower Jim. He dropped the shirt and ran for the business complex. It wouldn't hurt to pick up a few more of Kincaid's files for extra insurance.

The little window was still open. Jim climbed inside and jerked open the file cabinet. Not knowing what to take, he started stuffing everything into the bag.

"You've caused just about enough trouble!"

Jim didn't turn around. He knew it was Kincaid. He dropped the bag and ran for the window. Kincaid's aides were too fast for him. They pulled him out from behind the desk and held him firmly.

Kincaid's face darkened. "Take him to the medical lab. I'll do this one personally."

The aides dragged him down two long halls to the lab and strapped him to a narrow table. A nurse was ordered to administer an anesthetic.

In only a few minutes Jim could feel himself becoming drowsy. A bright light hanging from the ceiling was rocking back and forth, nearly blinding him.

Kincaid whistled as he put on his surgical

gloves. "This won't take long, Jim. I've decided to do a prefrontal lobotomy on you. It's been ages since I've done one. They frown on them now, you know. But it's the only way."

"You—you're crazy." Jim was having trouble staying awake.

Kincaid studied his tray of surgical tools. "You're lucky, really. When we find your little friend, she'll have to be done away with. Can't have any loose ends messing up our project."

Jim could feel himself going under.

In his delirium he could hear helicopters flying overhead, and he heard Maria talking. She took his hand and kissed him on the cheek.

What a wonderful dream.

CHAPTER 15

Sammy hopped up onto the couch in the Stantons' living room and crawled onto Laura's shoulder. "Look, Jimmy! He likes me."

Normally Jim would have made a sarcastic comment. But it had been only a week since the federal authorities had closed down Folsum National Laboratories, and he was just glad to have his sister back to normal.

"That's great, squirt. Take good care of him. He's a hero."

Jim's father slapped him on the back. "You're the hero, son. You and Maria."

His mother beamed with pride.

Max loudly cleared his throat.

Robert Stanton smiled. "And, of course, you too, Max. If you hadn't already called the police and made up that story about Maria's being kidnapped, help might not have gotten to Jim in time."

"It was nothing." Max feigned humility. "I was worried about those two being inside the compound so long and jumped the gun. I knew firsthand what kind of man Kincaid was. He'd stop at nothing to have his way."

Maria was strangely quiet. She stood up and excused herself. Jim heard the back door slam and rose to follow her.

He found Maria by the back gate, staring at the mountains.

"Hey, why so glum, Maria? We came out on top. My folks are okay. The people at the labs are all back to normal, and Kincaid and company are behind bars. What more could you ask for?"

She ran her finger along the edge of the fence. "Now that the lab is closed, I guess you and your family will be moving back to California."

Jim shook his head. "My dad and a couple of the other scientists have offered to stay here and work with the government to get the lab back on its feet."

"Really?" Maria tried not to sound too excited. "That's good . . . I mean, I was kinda looking forward to having someone to play baseball with." She opened the gate and slipped through.

"Baseball?" Jim touched his cheek and blushed bright red. He watched her walk up the hill and yelled after her, "Maria, I've been meaning to ask you something about the day you rescued me."

She looked back over her shoulder and smiled mischievously. "It was all just a dream, Young Frankenstein. Race you to the tunnel!"

"A dream?"

A big grin spread across his face.

He started running.

GARY PAULSEN
ADVENTURE GUIDE

MIND CONTROL SURVIVAL

When you hear the words *mind control,* what's the first thing that pops into your head? Do you think of things like hypnosis, drugs, and shock therapy? Those are obvious forms of mind control. But there are less noticeable forms that you probably experience every day.

When you see a television commercial for the newest sneakers worn by the biggest basketball star, do you *have* to have them, no matter what they cost? Do you ever do things you don't really feel like doing, just because your friends talk you into it? Well, then, you've experienced mind control. You've probably used it yourself on your parents when you've wanted something—like those new shoes—really badly.

Mind control involves changing a person's attitude and usual behavior. When someone tries to use mind control on you, it means they are trying to make you do or think what they want you to, which can be dangerous.

If you think someone is using mind control, you should analyze the message that's being sent. Ask the following questions: *Who* is sending the message? *What* is the message and to whom are they sending it? *How* are they sending the message, and most importantly, *why* are they sending this message?

How do you avoid mind control? The answer is simple. Think for yourself. Be your own person. No one can control what happens in your mind better than you.